A FOOLISH PRIDE

A PRIDE AND PREJUDICE VARIATION

BELLE REEVES

Four Rivers Press

1

ELIZABETH

"Must you leave now?"

My elder sister's moan was tinged with frustration. A regimental ball loomed on the horizon, and we both knew that would bring a great deal of noise and confusion to the house that our father would avoid at all costs and that our mother would only exacerbate. As the eldest daughters in a house of five, Jane and I had taken on many of the responsibilities that would typically fall to our mother.

But our mother was... well... She was incapable of such things, and I suspected that was by design more than anything. Jane and I were responsible and level-headed, more from necessity than anything. But the other girls, especially the younger two, seemed to be intent on following in our mother's footsteps.

"You know as well as I that our aunt and uncle have been promising to take me into the Lake Country for nigh on two years now," I said, "and I intend to make them keep their promise... You are not cross with me, are you?"

Jane sighed heavily. "No, Lizzy, of course not. It is just...

not the right time. The regimental ball— You know how the girls can be."

My smile felt more like a grimace. "I do, indeed. All too well."

"And Lydia is intent on dancing with every officer in the garrison just to vex Kitty, I am certain of that."

"There is little that I might accomplish with my presence if that is her goal," I said as I sank down onto the couch beside my sister. "I shall spend all of my hours between now and my departure making ribbon roses... would that please you?"

Jane laughed. "Only if you are making them for me, and I have no need of ribbon roses. I will miss your deft fingers — I have no doubt that Lydia will wish to have her sleeves changed only hours before we are set to leave... I cannot bear the stress of it!"

I draped my arm over my sister's stiff shoulder and hugged her tight. "You could come with me," I said brightly. "I am certain that you would enjoy the views, and our aunt has planned some delightful stops along the way—"

"You know I cannot do that," Jane said. "Mama is already bereft that you will be leaving us just when you are needed most."

"I am always needed most," I muttered.

"This is very true," Jane said with a rueful smile as she shrugged away from my arm. "I have a great deal to prepare," she said. "You could make yourself useful and assist me with choosing what I shall wear to the ball. I am certain that I will not have time to choose for myself before it is too late, and you know I make all the wrong decisions when I am pressed for time."

"Never fear," I declared. " We shall find you the most

wonderful gown, and it shall be you who dances with the entire regiment while Lydia watches from the sidelines."

Jane's laugh was genuine, and I felt a little less guilty... But only a little.

We had both spent far too many years watching our younger sisters dance with the officers and gentlemen who should have been our partners. I did not begrudge them the attention, I had come to peace with the possibility that one of our younger sisters would be the first among us to marry. But I was not certain that Jane had come to the same conclusion. Or if she was, in fact, ready to admit that such a thing was possible.

"I must pack," I said. "Let us choose your gown now, perhaps there is something among my things that you would like to borrow for the ball?"

"Your dresses are too short for me," Jane said with a frown, "but I have long admired the blue enamel flower pins that you have been wearing in your hair..."

"Of course," I exclaimed. "They would match your eyes perfectly."

As I followed Jane up to the bedchamber I shared, I hoped that I could do enough to ensure that my absence would not be too keenly felt. Lydia and Kitty seemed to have a talent for making every moment seem like an eternity. Even Mary, who claimed to prefer to be left alone, could be equally frustrating in her refusals to participate in any way.

It was Kitty and Lydia who swept up the most attention in the house, with Lydia being the mastermind behind every scheme and excuse for their bad behavior. They were not *bad* girls, not really, but I often worried that they would find themselves in more trouble than they could handle. It was why Jane and I kept such a close eye upon them—Lydia's selfishness was one of my main vexations, but it was also why I was so concerned for her. Her actions could lead Kitty into a terrible situation as well, and I did not wish that for her. Kitty was a sweet girl, and despite being older than Lydia by almost two years, she seemed to crave her sister's approval and attention... It was a cycle I did not believe I would be able to break on my own.

Perhaps, in time, Kitty would see that she could be special and important *without* Lydia's approval, but I could not know when that might occur... or if it were even possible.

*A*s I packed my valise and helped Jane to sift through her collection of gowns, of which there were not many that had not been re-hemmed, re-fitted, and re-sewn several times, I felt the guilt of leaving begin to lift away. The regimental balls, while entertaining in their own way, were not something that I enjoyed.

There were never enough partners to go around, and I found that much of my time was spent sitting and waiting for the gentlemen and officers to finish with their dances. While Mama might have been excited at the prospect of having a handsome officer as a husband for one of her daughters, I could not commit myself to the idea of being a soldier's wife.

Such a thing would have suited Lydia or Kitty very well, but they were young and silly, and I needed a husband that I could talk to—one that would not mind that I spent too much time reading, or that I played the pianoforte very ill. A husband who would not wish for me to sing when guests came to dinner, and one who would not expect that I would be anything but myself.

Jane would make an excellent wife for any man of gentle

breeding—she was lovely, kind, soft-spoken, and could play and sing beautifully. She could even speak French and her needlepoint was effortlessly exquisite.

Perhaps I would be a better wife for a lawyer, someone who might enjoy an amiable argument about a poem or a snatch of political writing... Or perhaps even a merchant who would take me abroad...

No soldiers for me.

No, indeed.

I fasted my valise and set it on the floor beside my bed.

"The mail coach will come tomorrow morning," I said, and Jane sighed heavily as she lifted the gown she had chosen to her shoulders to look at her reflection in the vanity mirror.

"I shall not be gone for too long," I continued. "It will only be a few weeks. You will scarcely notice that I am gone."

"*I* shall notice," Jane said. "Of course. And not just because Kitty and Lydia will drive me to distraction."

"I shall write to you," I promised. "Our aunt has told me that we shall be visiting several estates, as well as the one where she spent much of her childhood."

"It will be a wonderful journey," Jane said with a smile. "Of that I have no doubt. I shall look forward to your letters, but you must forgive me if mine are filled with moaning and complaints about our dear sisters."

Elizabeth laughed. "I expect to hear all about the regimental ball—knowing just how many officers, and of what quality they might be. Something that I am certain will be an all-important detail that our mother will speak about with endless obsession."

"Endless," Jane repeated and then she laughed again. "I will do my best to relay the details as faithfully as possible. I am certain that Lydia and Kitty will point out the most handsome young men whether or not I might wish to know."

"Do you not wish to have a handsome officer for yourself," I teased.

Jane made a face and laid the gown down upon her bed. "I have not yet decided," she said. "While it would seem an easy option, the garrison welcomes new officers every autumn... If I looked hard enough I am certain I might find one that would make Mama happy."

"But one that would make *you* happy," I said. "Is that not the whole aim of a marriage?"

Jane shrugged. "I am not certain what I believe," she said. "Our own parents do not seem anything but at odds. I like to believe that they had a great love story, but I do not think such a beginning would have resulted in what we see today."

"I cannot help but agree. I have long held up our aunt and uncle as an example of what I should like my own marriage to be," I said.

"Indeed?" Jane seemed amused by my admission, but it was the truth.

"I shall not marry for any tepid affection," I said firmly. "No convenience, no accident of fate... It shall be for a deep love that will stand the test of time. I am determined in that."

"And if you should never meet a gentleman who represents such a requirement?"

"Then I shall wait," I said. "If it is not to be, then I shall be an old maid and care for the children that my sisters bring into the world. I shall be an exemplary aunt and governess."

Jane laughed and sat down on her bed. "I should be very glad of such assistance when the time comes for me to marry. If nothing else, I shall be happy for your company."

I reached for Jane's hand and she gripped my fingers tightly.

The knowledge that we would be separated when one of us were married weighed heavily on my shoulders. I could not imagine what it would be like not to wake up and see Jane's sleeping form in her bed. Or laying awake in the dark listening to her even breathing. Or laughing together over the antics of our younger sisters... Everything would change.

I was not ready for such a thing.

Perhaps Jane was not ready, either.

~

*L*ondon... Jane was not certain of how she felt about the city, but I found it exciting. There was always so much movement in London, and even though the skies above were clouded and rain was an ever present threat, I still relished my time there.

Mrs. Gardiner had spent her girlhood in the countryside we were on our way to visit, but she loved the city as though she had been born to it. My own mother, who had spent much of her life before she met my father in London, had no such affinity for it, and I often wondered why that might be. Mr. Gardiner enjoyed the countryside, but the city was where he had always said he truly felt alive, and I supposed I felt similarly.

Mrs. Gardiner was already waiting in the carriage, and I smiled at the footman who lifted my valise onto the roof with the other trunks and bags that would accompany us north.

"Are you ready, Lizzy," my aunt called from her seat.

"I am," I replied as I refused the driver's offer of assistance to step up into the carriage.

"I do hope that you will forgive the delay in making this journey a reality," my aunt said with some chagrin. "It could not have been helped. My son—"

I smiled as I settled into the seat across from my aunt. "I know," I said. "It is not everyday that a young man sets off on a Grand Tour. I can imagine that it must have been stressful for you."

"It was," she exclaimed. "And your uncle very nearly decided to join him!"

"And I would have," Mr. Gardiner laughed from outside the carriage. "But I could not leave my poor bride behind in London all alone in that house." He climbed into the carriage and took hold of his wife's hand. He pressed it to his lips, making Mrs. Gardiner's cheeks flush pink as he winked at her.

This was what I wanted from my marriage—a love that would last. The very deepest love that could only grow and change over time. Perhaps it was an impossible demand, but if my aunt and uncle had found it, such a thing might be waiting for me.

I just had to find it.

2

ELIZABETH

*S*ilverwood was a fine example of a Derbyshire estate just on the border of Lambton, not far from the inn, and Mrs. Gardiner was the very picture of joy with every day we spent in the countryside she had been born in.

Mr. Gardiner, was, of course, just as pleased to be permitted to fish in the well-stocked lake on the estate's grounds, and I was content to prowl the libraries and corridors of the great house. It was a good deal larger than Longbourn, and I wondered how any young woman could be comfortable as the mistress of such a large house. It was something I had not thought of until recently—my own mother had done nothing to prepare any of us for such an eventuality.

She wanted very much for us to be married, but it was what came after the marriage that plagued me the most.

It was one thing to secure an engagement, but entirely another to actually *be* a wife. Lydia laughed endlessly about what would happen in the marriage bed, and I wondered who it was she had been speaking to about such things.

Perhaps her association with Colonel Forster's young wife was ill advised.

I knew little else about the young woman beyond the fact that she had married the Colonel quite unexpectedly, and I could only imagine what might have prompted such a choice. Whatever the reason, her influence on Lydia was cause for concern, and something I would have to better investigate when I returned to Hertfordshire.

The current residents of Silverwood were Mrs. Gardiner's cousins, the Darrow family, had welcomed us in with open arms. Miss Claudia Darrow, the eldest daughter, was only a year younger than myself, and she was a daring girl who loved to ride through the Derbyshire woods at speeds that frightened me just a little—it was thrilling, but I was not as confident in the saddle as I should have liked to be.

We had spent many diverting weeks in the countryside, which was at the same time so familiar and yet strange. At any moment in Lambton, I expected to come around a corner and see a familiar face from Meryton. I had never felt such comfort in London, or Bath, or any other place I had visited.

As she had promised, Jane had written to tell me of what was happening in Hertfordshire, and while I missed her greatly, I couldn't not deny that I was reluctant to return to the chaos of Longbourn and my mother's never ending search for any gentlemen who might consider making an offer of marriage to one of her daughters.

But return we must, for Mr. Gardiner had business to return to, and Mrs. Gardiner was due to host a salon for one of her ladies' groups.

Miss Darrow was adamant, however, that I should remain with them at Silverwood for another fortnight, and I found it difficult to decline her offer.

"But you must stay," Claudia exclaimed. "Ebony has just gotten used to your riding style, and I shall not be satisfied until you are able to best me in a race through the woods!"

Her pronouncement was met with laughter, and my cheeks were hot with pleased embarrassment as I tried to think of a way to protest... but I found that I could not.

"There is nothing pulling me back to Hertfordshire but the approach of the Meryton Assembly," I said, "but I do not feel any particular need to attend... Jane will forgive me in time."

"But you must invite her to come north as well," Claudia cried. It would be impossible, of course, but her invitation was eager enough to bring a smile to my face.

"You should stay," Mrs. Gardiner said. "I have kept you wrapped up in my own nostalgic delights for far too long. And you have made a good friend in Claudia."

I could not disagree with my aunt's assessment, but she had not bored me with her plans for the trip, and I had truly enjoyed every moment of it.

"Your nostalgic delights have kept all of us entertained," I said. "But I would be delighted to stay, if it will not be too much of an imposition on—"

I had scarcely uttered the words when they were interrupted by Claudia's shriek of joy. "But of *course* it will be no trouble," she cried. "Mama and Papa will be so pleased to have you stay, if only to keep me out of trouble and away from the house. Is that not so?"

Mr. and Mrs. Darrow did not protest their daughter's outburst, and I felt no small amount of pleasure to have been singled out in such a manner.

Much to my dismay, the Gardiners did not linger long after the announcement of my remaining at Silverwood.

Claudia was determined to distract me from the sudden melancholy brought on by my aunt's departure and she insisted that we take a turn through the garden to visit her mother.

Mrs. Darrow was seated in Silverwood's rose gardens, taking in the afternoon sunshine from the shelter of a large parasol.

"Ah, girls," Mrs. Darrow said, "as Miss Bennet will be staying with us for a little while longer, I should ask what it is you plan to do?"

"To do?" Claudia laughed. "Mama, you should not ask such things. We shall approach Miss Bennet's visit one wonderful say at a time. Is that not enough?"

"Surely, there is something that you would like to accomplish while you are here," Mrs. Darrow said with a smile. "There must be a reason for you to stay behind."

"A reason beyond my own desire to have a companion?" Claudia exclaimed.

"But you cannot expect that Miss Bennet will not have something she must return to in Hertfordshire," her mother protested.

"I have none," I replied. "I have my sisters, of course, but there is nothing calling me back to Hertfordshire at this moment. Even if there were... It would not be as though I might attend the Assembly."

"But you must be looking for a husband," Mrs. Darrow exclaimed, her voice teasing.

"A husband!" Claudia piped up. "Of course, Miss Bennet wishes to marry! Oh, do not let me keep you from such an opportunity. You must tell me all about the eligible young men in Hertfordshire, Lizzy!"

I laughed and shook my head. There was no way for me

to explain to them that the idea of marriage held very little appeal for me. The only eligible gentlemen I knew of in Hertfordshire were barely of age, and my mother was already obsessed with the idea of a match between Jane and the son of Mr. Bennet's solicitor... but he was hardly the sort of gentleman that Jane would be happy spending her life with.

"My presence at the Assembly is only required by my mother to ensure that her ambitions are realized."

"Of course, your mother wishes for you to marry," Mrs. Darrow said. "It is the dearest wish of every mother to see her daughters well taken care of."

It was impossible to miss the pointed nature of Mrs. Darrow's words, and the expression on Claudia's face was evidence enough that she did not appreciate her mother's suggestions.

"Surely, you have no objections to the idea of marriage?" Mrs. Darrow said.

"Only that I have not yet met the gentleman I wish to marry," I replied, "and while I am sure that he exists, I am equally sure that I shall not find him in Hertfordshire."

Claudia nodded in agreement. "We, of course, would not want to see Miss Bennet tied to a man she does not truly love."

From the direct manner of Claudia's statement, I could only suppose that Claudia had turned down more than one proposal that did not meet such a requirement.

"Surely, Mama, there might be a gentleman in Derbyshire who might meet with Miss Bennet's approval," Claudia continued thoughtfully.

"I have no doubt of that," I replied, "but it is hardly something that has given me sleepless nights. I am quite happy, I thank you."

"Nonsense," Mrs. Darrow said. "Leave it with me, Miss Bennet, I have no doubt that I might be able to locate such a gentleman without much effort."

Claudia's nose wrinkled. "Not one of my cast-off gentlemen, Mama," she said. "I beg you, give Miss Bennet leave to have a fortnight of relaxation free of maternal scheming!"

Claudia's words were good-natured, but I couldn't help but wonder if Claudia was also benefiting from my presence at Silverwood. She was certainly of a marriageable age, but she seemed as uninterested in matrimony as I was.

"I shall take Miss Bennet to the stables, I think," Claudia declared before her mother could say anything more. "Come, Lizzy, we shall have the wind in our hair and forget our mothers and their mysterious plans for our future."

I thanked Mrs. Darrow once more for their hospitality as Claudia grabbed hold of my arm and pulled me in the direction of the stables.

~

"I confess I have not as much experience in the saddle as I should like," I admitted as the stables came into view.

"You need not worry," Claudia replied, "I will take good care of you. Once you have seen the horses, however, I think you shall change your mind."

Silverwood's stables were well appointed and it was clear that Mr. Darrow took great pride in the beasts that roamed the fields and whickered softly as we approached.

The horses were of noble bearing and no expense had been spared with their care. They were a variety of colors, but

I thought them all beautiful. Their coats were brushed to a lustrous sheen, and their manes shimmered like silk. They were the most beautiful things I had ever seen.

Within moments, Claudia proved that she was as competent in the stables as she was at the card tables. I had no trouble taking Claudia's word that she knew how to ride. It was impossible for me to imagine my mother, or even Jane and Kitty, venturing out into the stables. My father kept a very poor stable in comparison to this one.

Claudia and I each chose a mount and the stable lads rushed to secure their saddles and fit the bridles into their mouths. I couldn't help but admire Claudia's prowess as she checked the straps on her saddle and then mine before she flung off her bonnet and gloves and easily mounted her horse.

"Come along, Lizzy," she cried. "You will be just fine. Do exactly as I do!"

She set her heels into the stirrups, riding astride like a men, and took off at a quick gallop.

I had never ridden a horse as tall and powerful as the one I was trying to mount, but I was not about to let that stop me.

"Good girl," I whispered as I stroked the mare's mane.

It was the first time I had ridden astride, and it felt strange in my gown. I wished that I had worn something a little warmer, for the weak autumn sunlight provided little comfort, and if we were to ride as quickly as I suspected Claudia would wish to, I would be chilled to the bone in no time at all.

With as much confidence as I could muster, I took hold of the reins and nudged the horse into a trot to catch up with Claudia.

Claudia's grin was infectious and I felt some of my nervousness ebb away.

"We shall race!" she cried out. "To the fence!"

It was not a long race, and Claudia was easily able to pull ahead of me, but I did not begrudge her the victory. My concentration was on keeping pressure on the reins, and myself upright in the saddle.

"Shall we race again?" she called out as I came through a stand of silver trunked birch trees that gave the estate its name.

I couldn't say no to another race. Every moment in the saddle brought me more confidence and I didn't want to lose the feeling of it.

It was not long before Claudia and I were racing across the hills and fields of Silverwood and away across the neighboring estate's acres. The wind whipped my hair back and the sun warmed my cheeks. I had never felt so free.

The stables were well out of sight and I could barely discern the direction we had come from when Claudia finally slowed her gelding to a walk.

"I can understand why you love to ride," I said as I wiped the sweat from my brow and reined in my mare. "It is just... wonderful."

"I am glad to hear it," she replied. "I wish that I could persuade my mother to ride more often. She is quite afraid of the horses and the stable lads. I cannot understand it. She would become much better acquainted with our people if she came with me, but I suspect she believes it not to be of much importance."

"You must find a husband who enjoys the thrill of riding as much as you do," I said.

Claudia laughed. "Perhaps. And what of you, Lizzy?

What sort of gentleman would you prefer? A hunter? A gamesman? Surely not a stuffy old law clerk or a merchant?"

I shook my head. "None of them," I sighed. "I have not, truthfully, given much thought to *what* sort of gentleman my husband might be, only that I would know as soon as I met him that he would be the only companion that my heart desired. That is all."

"That is all," Claudia mocked me gently. "Such a simple request. My dear, Lizzy, I do not know if young ladies such as ourselves can hope for so much."

"Perhaps not," I replied ruefully. "But one can wish for such things."

"Only in the darkest hours of the night," Claudia said and I couldn't mistake the hint of bitterness in her words. *Did Mrs. Darrow have plans for Claudia's future that she did not agree with?*

But Claudia did not give me a chance to ask any other questions as she spurred her gelding into a trot once more.

"Let us ride down to the lake," she declared. "Then we shall head back to the estate. It should be almost supper time, and I shall be wanting a bath before we rejoin the household."

"Indeed," I laughed. I had forgotten the cold, but as we had walked the horses, I had been reminded of the sharpness of the wind.

Over the hills, an unexpected bank of dark clouds had built and threatened foul weather as it approached.

"One more race," I agreed. "But we should keep an eye on the weather... Papa did tell me that the almanac predicted some wilder weather as winter approached."

"No wild weather shall keep me from beating you in

another race," Claudia cried. She set her heels into her horse's flanks and the gelding leapt forward.

I let out a furious breath as the first drops of rain began to fall.

"One more," I muttered as I gritted my teeth, took hold of the reins and pressed my heels into the mare's flanks to mirror Claudia's confident movements.

The mare jumped forward into a trot and transitioned almost immediately into a canter that took my breath away.

I had no time to think about how fast we were going as the spattering rain drops quickly became a deluge, soaking me through to my skin in seconds as the horse tore across the field.

My heart was in my throat as I tried to keep my seat, but it was all I could do to hang on.

"Slow down," I pleaded, but I was drowned out by the pounding of hooves and the pounding of the rain.

Claudia had pulled ahead of me and I could only hear the beats of her horse's hooves, and her laughter as the gelding tore through the field and plunged into the trees as she continued to race ahead of me.

I urged my horse to go faster, but the mare was already pushing herself to the limits as she thundered through the muddy grass.

"Claudia," I cried out. But I knew that she could not hear me over the storm. The wind had picked up and the rain was coming down in torrents.

I tried to keep pace with her, but her gelding was too fast and I could barely control my own mount.

As we plunged into the forest, I felt a brief sense of relief as the trees blocked the worst of the rain, but then, with a sudden sickening lurch, the mare twisted, throwing me from the saddle.

It all happened so quickly, I didn't even have time to scream. Instead, I was left gasping for air as I lay on the forest floor with the pounding of the mare's hooves in my ears and the raging wail of the wind as it howled through the trees. The branches twisted above me, blurring in my vision until tears streamed from my eyes. I closed them for just a moment, but the blackness that had loomed behind the trees swept over me and dragged me away.

3

DARCY

*T*he mare was riderless, nostrils wide and eyes rolling with fear as I caught sight of her. She had burst from the trees on the far side of the estate, and if I had not been speaking to the gamekeeper, I would not have found her.

The unexpected storm lashed me with rain as I ran across the field toward the horse.

"What happened to you, my beauty?" I murmured as I caught hold of her bridle and tried to calm the frightened beast.

Riderless.

There was a scrap of fabric caught in a buckle on the mare's saddle and I plucked it from the metal to inspect it more closely. Patterned muslin. This was not a gentleman's horse—but that could only mean that someone was injured...

The sudden thought was painful, and I quickly adjusted the straps and buckles on the mare's saddle to accommodate the length of my legs.

Whoever had been riding her previously had been quite small in stature, and I could not imagine what might have happened...

I swung up into the saddle and turned the mare in the direction from which she had come.

There was a narrow road through the forest that led toward the neighboring estates, and I wondered briefly which one she had come from.

The mare reared back and almost refused to re-enter the woods, but I held her steady and urged her forward.

The forest road was well traveled, but there was another track, one I had not used before, and a freshly broken tree branch signaled that was the way the mare had come.

I turned the mare to my right and nudged her into a gentle trot along the path.

The track was overgrown and dense with shrubbery and brambles that scratched at me as I passed, and I was forced to duck beneath low-hanging branches. The trail wound through the forest, and I had just begun to wonder if I had made the right choice when I caught a flash of white among the greenery.

I slowed the mare and eased her along the overgrown trail before bringing her to a stop.

I jumped down from the saddle and pulled the mare along behind me as I pushed through the underbrush. The flash of white had been the edge of a young woman's skirts. She lay on her stomach in the mud, her dark hair wet and plastered across her cheek. She was not dressed for riding, but for walking in a garden on an autumn day.

How had she come to be here so unprepared?

I looked around, hoping to catch sight of a companion, or

other person nearby, but there was no sign of anyone else and the only noise in the forest was the rushing of the wind through the trees and the roar of the storm.

"Miss..." I dropped to my knees at the young woman's side. "Miss, can you hear me?"

She moved her head slightly, moaning at the touch of my hand upon her shoulder. There was blood on her hand, and more on her scalp just as her hairline. A thin trickle of it snaked down her cheek.

Without thinking, I gathered the young woman into my arms and lifted her out of the mud. The horse pranced with nervous fear, but I quieted her as best I could as I laid the young woman across the saddle.

I would take her back to Pemberley--Mrs. Reynolds would know what to do. And Dr. Mason would have to be called from Lambton.

Holding the mare steady, I mounted slowly so as not to cause her to panic and held the unconscious young woman tight against my chest as I settled into the saddle. If nothing else, the warmth of my body might bring her around... I had no thought for anything but to get her back to the house.

Pemberley was not far, but the storm and mud made it seem much farther. I kicked the mare into a trot, and tried not to think about what I must look like as I pressed the young woman against me. She was very small, as I had guessed, and her weight was nothing against me.

I felt some relief to see Pemberley's graceful walls through the trees, and urged the horse faster.

As we approached the house, the front doors opened and Mrs. Reynolds stood in the doorway as two footmen rushed out to assist me.

One footman pulled the young woman from my arms and

I shouted for them to take her into the house as the other took hold of the mare's reins. I jumped down from the saddle and gave the mare over to the footman as I charged into the house. I swept the nameless rider into my arms once more, intent on getting my charge inside and dry, then into the hands of a doctor.

"Darcy! What in heaven's name!"

Charles Bingley, his eyes wide with surprise, stood in the corridor. "You are soaking wet! Did you go out in that storm? And who is that?"

"I did, and I do not know," I replied tersely. "Mrs. Reynolds, which room--"

"The Rose Room, I should think," the housekeeper answered quickly. "I shall send word to Dr. Mason."

"Quickly," I said. "And send up a maid with some washing water, she is covered in mud. One of Georgiana's sleeping robes should fit her well enough."

The housekeeper nodded and hurried toward the stairs that led to the second floor.

"Did you find her in the forest?" Bingley asked, aghast.

"I did," I replied as I followed Mrs. Reynolds. "She's injured. A fall from her horse as she took shelter from the storm. The beast must have been spooked and thrown her."

"How awful," he exclaimed. "And you do not know who she might be?"

"I do not," I called back over my shoulder. I looked down into her face, smeared with mud and the blood from her injury. She was beautiful, despite it all, and something tugged at my heart as I shifted her slight frame in my arms.

"I shall be down shortly," I said. "Inform your sisters that we shall have another guest in the house."

"They will not take kindly to it," Charles snorted. "Even

tragically unexpected guests are still the worst kind..."

"Indeed."

The Rose Room had been out of use for some time and was slightly dusty, but it was clean and the bed had been freshly made. I carried the young woman in and placed her on the embroidered coverlet.

"Who is she?" Charles asked as he entered the room. I did not have an answer.

"I do not recognize her as being from one of the neighboring estates," I said. "I cannot say."

"Is she badly injured?"

"I do not think so. The wound on her head seems small, but the gash on her hand will need a doctor's care. I think her wrist might be broken, but I could not tell."

"That's a shame," Charles said, shaking his head. "She's a pretty little thing. Dr. Mason is on his way, I trust?"

"I have sent a footman on horseback," Mrs. Reynolds said brightly. "Now, gentlemen, if you will excuse me, I shall look after this young woman until the doctor arrives."

I nodded, but was still unwilling to leave, though I knew that I had to. "Of course, do keep me informed of her condition."

"I shall, of course, Mr. Darcy," she replied with a smile. "Now, off with you. This young lady has been through an ordeal and she is getting the coverlet muddy and I must correct that."

Charles grabbed hold of my elbow to pull me toward the door, and we dodged out of the way as three maids carrying hot washing water and clean linens swept into the room.

In the corridor, Charles slapped his hand against my back. "You're soaking wet, Darcy," he exclaimed.

I was. Though I had hardly noticed it until that precise moment.

"I shall have to change--"

"You must, or Caroline will talk of nothing else."

~

I would not have mattered how carefully I dressed, Caroline Bingley would always have a sharp word of judgment. It was fortunate that I was not affected by how capriciously Miss Bingley's favor waxed and waned.

Charles, however, took much of her criticism to heart. Especially when it came to the young ladies who might become the future Mrs. Bingley.

As I walked through the corridor toward the parlor where Caroline and Louisa were currently holding court, I briefly entertained the thought of going back out into the rain and down to the stables.

The young lady who lay upstairs awaiting the ministrations of Dr. Mason had been plainly dressed, and I did not suppose that she might be the daughter of a wealthy household. Perhaps a servant, or the wife of a farmer...

"You saw it as plainly as I did, Louisa," Caroline exclaimed from the parlor. "The poor creature was a bedraggled mess. She must have fallen directly in a mud puddle to be so covered!"

"The poor creature must have fallen from her horse," Louisa observed. "But what could have possessed Mr. Darcy to bring her back to Pemberley?"

"You know as well as I do that Mr. Darcy is a sentimental sort of gentleman," Caroline sighed.

"Indeed, but I did supposed that he might be impervious to the charms of strange women," Louisa replied with a tinkling laugh. Even from the other side of the hallway, I could smell her overly sweetened perfume.

Going out into the rain seemed preferable to their company now.

Where was Charles?

"And such a mess," Louisa continued. "There was so much mud upon her face that I could not tell if she had a pretty face or not... and her hair was assuredly very dark. As dark as the mud."

"Did she have no bonnet, no cap?" Caroline asked.

I paused outside the door, unseen, and listened to their conversation.

"No, no hairpiece of any kind," Louisa replied. "So shameful to be caught improperly dressed. And not even in a proper riding habit! It looked as though she were wearing only a muslin dress!"

"A pitiful thing," Caroline agreed. "But I suppose her appearance was the least of her problems," Caroline said.

"Indeed," Charles blurted out.

Ah, so he *was* there.

"She was fortunate the Darcy found her," he continued. "She was injured, Caroline, I would expect you, both of you, to be kinder when she is able to join us."

"Join us," Caroline exclaimed. "Is she to be a guest here? I should think that Mr. Darcy would return her to whatever estate she is in service to as quickly as possible. Perhaps they will offer some compensation for the doctor's fees and the washing of her clothes."

"That is not your decision to make," Charles spluttered, and I decided that I'd had enough of listening to them.

I strode into the room and Caroline's sour expression brightened immediately as she laid eyes on me.

It was not lost on me that Caroline Bingley had designs on being the Mistress of Pemberley, but there was certainly no chance that I would ever be so desperate to a take a wife that I would consider her for the position.

"Now we might ask the gentleman himself," Caroline purred. "Mr. Darcy, wherever did you find that wet rag doll?"

I took the glass of whiskey that Charles held out for me with a grateful smile. "The young woman was injured," I said. "I found her horse wandering, riderless, along the border of the woods near the gamekeeper's cottage. I rode into the forest and found her, injured, on the ground. I couldn't very well just leave her there..."

"No, of course not," Louisa said with a condescending smile. "You must admit that it was quite a dramatic rescue. We were aghast when we saw you galloping toward the house!"

"And carrying her like-- Well." Caroline sipped her tea and watched me over the rim of her cup. I had some suspicion that she was attempting some kind of flirtation, but it would not work.

"I suppose there is nothing to be done about the clothes, unless one of the maids--"

"She is of a similar size to Georgiana," I interrupted. "I have given Mrs. Reynolds permission to clothe her from my sister's wardrobe."

Caroline's mouth fell open in surprise.

"But she is a servant," she said. "Surely--"

"We do not know that," I snapped. "She could be from one

of the neighboring estates. I would not assume who she might be just from one glance."

"And what of her injuries?" Louisa asked. "I thought I saw blood..."

"Once Dr. Mason has tended to her wounds we might be able to discover who she is, and where she came from. I should like to see her well on the road to recovery before thinking of sending her back onto the road."

Charles took a sip of whiskey and made a face. "Curse that doctor," he said bitterly. "Why must it take so long to attend to the slightest injury?"

"I do agree that a doctor should know what he is doing if he is to earn his money," Louisa interjected.

"We are not debating the value of doctors," I said mildly. "Dr. Mason has been a faithful caretaker to Pemberley's residents, and indeed, the surrounding estates. I shall be glad to have him here when he arrives. I trust that he shall put all of his efforts into seeing the young lady's injuries are taken care of."

"Of course," Louisa said soothingly, but Caroline made a face into her tea cup.

"He should arrive at any moment," I continued. "Mrs. Reynolds has promised to keep me informed of any changes..."

"And when she wakes up enough to tell you who she is," Caroline muttered.

"Indeed."

"And then we must talk of what we are to do for Christmas. I cannot abide a winter season in the country. Surely, Charles, you must listen to reason!"

Of course Caroline could not resist in turning the conversation back to her own concerns.

My own thoughts were drawn to how long it might take for Dr. Mason to arrive... and if the mysterious young woman upstairs in the Rose Room would recover from her injuries. Perhaps they were not as dire as he feared.

ELIZABETH

*M*y head ached, and my entire body felt as though I had been kicked out of a carriage and rolled roughly down a rocky hill.

I struggled to open my eyes, and realized that I did not recognize the room in which I was currently in—nor the nightgown that I wore.

What had happened?

"Oh— Oh, dear—"

"Now, now, Miss," a kindly older woman appeared at my side. "You just lie back. Dr. Mason says that you must rest. You struck your head quite hard when you fell."

"When I fell—" I murmured. "The mare—"

"Safely tucked away in our stables," the woman said. "You were most fortunate that my master found her and came into the woods to look for her rider. He found you in a most perilous situation, indeed!"

"I— I see—" embarrassment coursed through me as I remembered that I had lost my balance and fallen from the mare's back as she ran through the woods. "The storm—"

"It has not quite run its course," the woman said. "But the rain has tapered off somewhat. Are you warm enough?"

"I— Yes. I thank you," I managed.

"Good! Now, I'll just fetch a cool cloth for your brow, and put another log on the fire. Dr. Mason left me with strict instructions to bring down your fever and keep you as warm as possible. How the poor man keeps such things in order is beyond me, but I shall not fail in my duty!"

The woman bustled off, as though I were in the midst of a routine illness and that my life had not very recently been in danger. My arm was bandaged, wrapped in strips of white linen that felt stiff to the touch, I could only guess that the fabric had been starched to keep the limb somewhat immobile.

I pressed gently at it, testing for broken bones, but though every spot hurt, nothing felt out of place.

The older woman introduced herself as Mrs. Reynolds as she returned to the room and laid a cool cloth on my forehead. The pounding of my headache eased somewhat as I sank back onto the pillows and watched her bustle about the room.

I lay there, feeling the cool cloth on my forehead, listening to the sounds of the storm outside, and wondered what might have happened if the mysterious master of this estate had not noticed me sprawled in the mud.

"I have informed my master that you are awake," she said briskly as she laid another log upon the fire that crackled in the hearth.

"Oh-- May I ask, who is he? What is this estate?"

"This is Pemberley," the woman said proudly. "And my master is Mr. Fitzwilliam Darcy. His sister, Georgiana, is a few years younger than you, but she is not here at the moment."

"Oh."

I had hoped for some female companionship in my convalescence, but if--

"And Mrs. Darcy?"

Mrs. Reynolds smiled, somewhat sadly it seemed. "There is no Mrs. Darcy as yet," she said. "But I do hope that one day I shall see these corridors filled with laughter once more."

"Indeed," I murmured.

I heard footsteps in the corridor and tried to sit up straighter, but Mrs. Reynolds clucked and pushed me gently back onto the pillows.

"I trust that you are not too uncomfortable?" A gentleman's voice, warm and curious echoed in the room.

In the doorway, a tall gentleman with dark hair that curled over the collar of his jacket regarded me with a curious gaze. His dark eyes swept over me and lingered on the bandage on my arm.

"Not broken?"

"I do not think so," I replied.

"I am glad to hear it. Dr. Mason seems confident that you will be recovered very soon and will be able to return to your home."

"I— I must thank you," I said. "You saved my life."

"Nonsense," he said with a dismissive wave of his hand. "I only did what anyone would have done."

"It is more than that," I said. "You came to look for me... If you had not--"

I did not want to say that no one would have found me, but the truth of it was clear enough to us both.

"You are very welcome," he said, still looking down on me with a curious gaze. "But let us say no more about that. Tell me, who are you, and how did you come to be in the woods in such a storm?"

"My name is Elizabeth Bennet. I am from Hertfordshire... but I am staying with my aunt's cousin at Silverwood Estate."

His eyes widened. "Hertfordshire... I cannot say that it is a part of the country that I have visited. I do, however, know of the Silverwood Estate. I shall send a note immediately so that they know where you are and will tell them not to worry for your safety."

"Thank you," I said, with a small smile of gratitude.

"Though you have not said how you came to be in such a storm. It was not weather for a casual afternoon ride.The storm was quite fierce."

"Indeed," I replied. "It swept over me without warning," I said. "I have never seen such a storm. It seemed as though it had come out of nowhere."

"Were you traveling with a companion?" he asked.

"I was... Miss Claudia Darrow."

"I am surprised that they did not send anyone to search for you. You have been at Pemberley for three days now."

I bit my lip. *Had it really been so long? Why had they not come to look for me?*

"But the storm has been raging these last days, so you must not blame them," he said as though he could read my thoughts.

"Is there anyone else you would like to write to?" he asked kindly.

"Yes," I replied immediately. "My sister. If it would not be too much trouble. I should like to let her know what happened, she will have been expecting me to return to Hertfordshire within a few days, she does not know that I was to stay on at Silverwood for another fortnight."

"Mrs. Reynolds will see that you have a writing desk," he said with a smile. "When you are feeling well enough, you will be welcome in the parlor. My friend from London, Mr. Charles Bingley, and his sisters, Miss Bingley and Mrs. Hurst, are also staying here, and they would be very pleased to meet you. I must admit they are quite curious about you. As was I."

His last words drew a surprised flush to my cheeks as I clutched at the embroidered coverlet.

"You have been very kind," I murmured.

"Come now, Sir," Mrs. Reynolds said, "you must allow her to rest. Dr. Mason would scold you like a schoolboy if he knew you were here."

"Of course," he chuckled. "Rest well, Miss Bennet. I do hope that we can speak again soon."

"As do I," I said and then felt instantly foolish as my cheeks heated once more.

Mrs. Reynolds chuckled as she pulled the coverlet up higher and patted my knee.

"I shall bring a writing desk," she said. "And you may write to your sister. We shall see that your letter is delivered."

"I thank you," I said. "You are very kind."

～

It was several days before the kindly Dr. Mason informed me that I was well enough to entertain company, the injury to my head had been slight, and my wrist was only sprained. The cut on my hand was beginning to heal, though it looked terrifying under its bandages.

Dr. Mason had apologized that I would have a scar, but reasoned that young ladies shouldn't have to worry about such things when wearing gloves in polite company. It seemed a flippant sort of reassurance, but it would have to be enough. My sisters and mother would have to forgive the blemish on my skin, but no one else would need to know.

Claudia was kind enough to send a letter to say how worried she had been, but she also mentioned that I would be in safe hands at Pemberley, and I wondered if I was imagining the teasing tone of her voice when it came to her mention of Mr. Darcy as one of the finest gentlemen in all of Derbyshire... Such a thing did not much matter to me.

Mrs. Reynolds was kind enough to bring me items from Mr. Darcy's sister's wardrobe that she had left behind. She apologized that they were not the latest fashions from London, but I had spent years in re-hemmed gowns with re-sewn sleeves and ribbons, and Georgiana Darcy's cast-off gowns were a luxury I did not expect to enjoy so much.

Dressed in a pale blue gown made of a finer material than I had ever possessed in my own wardrobe, I sat still while a maid deftly curled and arranged my hair into a style that was more befitting a daughter of a wealthy household than someone like me... It looked well, I could not deny it, but it felt somewhat disingenuous to be wearing another young lady's finery in a house that was not my own.

But I was a guest here, and I could not argue with my treatment. It was lovely... but it could not last forever.

Indeed, my idyllic impression of Pemberley was changed the moment I entered the parlor on Pemberley's main floor.

An elegant young woman dressed in a bright green gown sat on a plushly upholstered velvet couch across from another woman in a dark blue gown. They both wore countless pieces of jewellery and their hairstyles were elegant and regal. I could not imagine dressing in such finery for something as mundane as sitting down to tea on a Thursday afternoon.

Two tea settings had been placed in the room. One on a table near the gentlemen who read newspapers near the crackling fire, and one before the two women.

"Ah, Miss Eliza Bennet, I presume," the woman in green exclaimed. She rose from the couch in a fluid motion and approached me as a cat might approach a mouse.

"Caroline," the other woman said. "You must give her a chance to sit down. We have heard all about you, Miss Bennet. All the way from Hertfordshire, is it? How quaint."

It was clear that I was not going to be introduced to the other women, so I could only guess that the younger of the two was Miss Caroline Bingley, and the elder was Mrs. Hurst.

I curtseyed as was proper, but Caroline merely rolled her eyes in response as she returned to her seat upon the couch.

"You must forgive my sister," Mrs. Hurst said. "Please, come and sit down. I wish to hear all about you and your life in Hertfordshire."

I did as instructed and took a seat upon a chair directly across from Caroline Bingley, who regarded me with an icy stare.

I looked down at the tea service in an attempt to distract myself. A teacup and saucer had been set out for me, and my stomach tightened at the sight of a plate of sweet pastries and shortbread. *Was I even hungry?*

"Mr. Darcy tells us that your arrival at Pemberley was most harrowing," Mrs. Hurst began. She leaned forward to pour me a cup of tea and I smiled gratefully.

"The storm was, indeed, very frightening," I said. "I was racing my friend, Claudia--"

"Racing?" Caroline snorted. "How unladylike! You were not even dressed for riding! How did such a thing happen?"

"It was quite accidental," I said.

"You seem prone to such things," Caroline observed.

I frowned at her.

What was she implying?

"I am not as confident a rider as my companion," I said.

"That is what I might have expected," Caroline said with a smile that seemed more mocking than genuine. "I would have thought you were more of the type to sit at home, reading a book."

"What does my love of horses have to do with my reading habits, pray tell," I asked.

"Though I do not know you, Miss Eliza, it is quite easy to make assumptions. How old are you?"

"One-and-twenty," I replied.

"And how many sisters have you?"

"Four."

"Goodness," she exclaimed. "And are any of them married? Surely the eldest must be by now..."

"No," I replied.

Caroline's mouth pinched. "A pity. It is well known that a young lady with fine eyes and a sharp wit might secure herself a husband with ease, unless of course there is some other defect in her personality..."

Mrs. Hurst looked between us with alarm. "Now, Caroline, Miss Bennet is a guest here at Pemberley. I should like to know more about what brought you here!"

"Indeed," the gentleman seated by the fire snapped his newspaper shut and jumped to his feet. "Have you not heard, Louisa, Mr. Darcy's rescue of Miss Bennet was most dramatic.

You would not think so to hear him tell it, but I found it quite harrowing!"

I was somewhat taken aback by the gentleman's enthusiasm. He began to pace the room, waving his hands as he spoke.

"Imagine! The storm, the horse stumbling... and then, after falling, Miss Bennet was bleeding profusely, lying in the mud unconscious. If Mr. Darcy had not found her horse and come back to find her... Well. And then he brought her back to Pemberley, riding at breakneck speed through the forest and across the fields in the driving rain before he carried her into the house. A most dramatic story, indeed, would you not agree?!"

"Oh, Charles," Caroline said with a roll of her eyes. "You are always telling some story of some horrid adventure. And how much of it is actually true?"

"It is all true," Mr. Darcy said from the fireside. He did not look up from his paper, but my cheeks warmed as he spoke. "Though Charles does tell it with a good deal more enthusiasm than might be required."

"I say, that is not true at all," Mr. Bingley exclaimed. "Her life was in danger! I shudder to think of what might have happened if you did not discover her mare wandering near the wood!"

"Ah, Charles," Darcy said with a shrug, "there is no need to exaggerate. It was just a mare... and Dr. Mason confirmed that Miss Bennet's injury was not that severe."

"Still, you saved her life," Mr. Bingley cried, "you were a true hero!"

Darcy shook his head, unwilling to accept such praise. "The credit belongs to the animal. I did what any man should have done."

"I daresay I would have done the same if I had found a beautiful young woman in the woods," he said with a sigh. "Although I might have been tempted to declare myself as a suitor for her hand had I known of her injury."

It was difficult not to laugh, for Mr. Bingley was so endearing and enthusiastic in his exclamations, much to the disdain of his sisters, which made it all the more amusing.

"Of course!" Caroline said sharply. "And then *you* would have been out in the rain in your nightclothes and your slippers, hunting for some wayward mare in the hopes that it would lead you to a bride!"

"And you would still find some reason to find fault with her," Charles retorted.

A tense silence fell over the parlor and I wished very much that I could just sink into the chair and disappear from it all.

"So, Miss Bennet. Five sisters all in one household, however does your mother manage?"

Grateful for a small distraction, I answered as best I could. The truth was uncomfortable, for my mother did not manage anything. We managed ourselves, but that was not a topic for polite conversation, especially with strangers.

"Is there a militia garrison in Hertfordshire," Caroline interjected.

"There is, indeed," I replied. "In Meryton, the town that is closest to our house there is a very active garrison. They winter in Hertfordshire and then march south to Brighton for the summer months."

"How thrilling for a house with five daughters," she said smoothly. "The soldiers do look so handsome in their uniforms, do they not?"

"I had not noticed," I replied, "though my younger sisters

would be hard-pressed to deny their interest in the young officers who come to town."

"Indeed." Caroline's smile was catlike and I did not like it one bit.

"And is there much society to be had?" she asked.

"Some. There are balls and assemblies, and my mother's friends are starting to show an interest in starting a salon for the young ladies of Hertfordshire to show off their accomplishments."

"And what are *your* accomplishments, Miss Eliza?" she purred. "We all know that you are not a horsewoman."

"I--"

I could not think of how to answer the question, which seemed more mocking than inquisitive.

Thankfully, I was spared giving a reply by the arrival of Mrs. Reynolds who carried a handful of letters. Two of them, as it happened, were for me, and I could not stop the small cry of joy that burst from my lips to see Jane's delicate handwriting.

At last. A reply.

5

DARCY

J hadn't been certain of how Miss Elizabeth Bennet's presence would be received by Mr. Bingley's sisters, but I was surprised, and pleased, by her ability to hold her own in conversation with them. They were snakes, but Miss Bennet was a deft wit, and she seemed not to be bothered or insulted by Caroline's biting observations and Louisa's condescension.

It was Charles who had surprised him the most. His friends was usually an excitable fellow, but he seemed very interested in the discovery of Miss Bennet after her accident, and appeared to wish that it had been *he* who had rescued the young lady instead.

I should not have felt any jealousy for such a thing, but the more time I spent in Miss Elizabeth Bennet's presence, the more I knew that I would have begrudged my friend such a privilege.

As we sat in the parlor and I did my utmost to ignore the conversation happening just a few feet away, it was the arrival of the letters that changed the entire mood of the room.

"Miss Eliza, I daresay your cheeks are quite pink, are you quite well?" Louisa exclaimed.

"I am," Elizabeth replied. "It is only... my sister. She has written two letters, each only a week apart, they must have been delayed in arriving. She was on her way to Silverwood Estate to meet me and stay with the Darrows, and then she has heard of my... calamity and she is coming to Pemberley with all haste."

"Here?" Caroline cried.

"Wonderful," Charles exclaimed. "Darcy, you would not refuse Miss Bennet's sister?"

"Of course not," I said. "I welcome her arrival. I shall be certain to have Mrs. Reynolds prepare a room for her."

"Goodness," Louisa said. "This is a time of new arrivals, is it not?"

"So it would seem," Caroline replied tersely.

"Mr. Darcy, you are too kind," Elizabeth said. "I promise that Jane and I will not stay long. I should like to return to Silverwood Estate, and then to Hertfordshire as soon as possible. You have been very generous, but I will not trespass on your kindness for much longer."

"Nonsense," I said. "Your presence has been no trouble at all. I have been in contact with the Darrow's, and they are happy that you have been well taken care of."

Elizabeth's cheeks flushed prettily and I felt a surge of something like affection in my chest. *Impossible.*

But perhaps.

No.

She would never do.

I had pretended not to know anything of Hertfordshire, but as she had spoken of her life with Caroline and Louisa, I had put the necessary pieces together. She was from a poor family with too many daughters and the likelihood that their mother was a grasping woman who would take every opportunity to shove her daughters in front of any eligible bachelor with five thousand a year was too great to chance.

All of the accomplishment and sharp wits in the world would not change any of that.

Caroline had called me arrogant on far too many occasions to ignore it. But even if she were correct, I owed it to Georgiana to make a wise choice of wife.

It was why I would never consider someone like Miss Elizabeth Bennet as the companion of my heart and hearth. Such arrangements always came with other problems.

Like extended family and other unwelcome relations.

"Well, Miss Eliza," Caroline huffed. "I do hope that your elder sister is as lovely as you."

It was exceedingly clear that Caroline did not hope for such a thing, and that she truly wished for Miss Bennet, and her sister who had not yet arrived, to depart as quickly as possible.

"I am *certain* of it," Louisa echoed with a smile that somehow seemed more disingenuous than her own sister's.

Charles said nothing, but then again nothing was needed to be said. The evidence was all over his face.

Miss Bennet smiled, but I could tell that she was embarrassed by Caroline's rudeness.

"Thank you, Miss Bingley," she said in a soft voice that I was certain that she only used when she did not want anyone to hear. "I am certain that Jane will be delighted to see the rolling hills of Derbyshire."

And that was enough to set Caroline off once more.

"Oh goodness, you do not find the Derbyshire country to be dreary?" Caroline exclaimed. "I could not bear the thought of being trapped here once the snow begins to fall! When it is not snowing, it is raining, and I cannot bear the thought of being trapped inside the house so far away from all the delights of London!"

"No, no, not dreary in the least," Elizabeth replied with a small smile. "I have always found the Derbyshire countryside to be quite beautiful. It is London that I find dreary and cold. The countryside will always be a home to me, no matter where in the country I might be."

Caroline let out a huff. "Indeed. I could not bear it. That is why we must plan to return to London well before Christmastime, is that not so, Charles?"

"Indeed," he replied. "I also know that you will not give me any peace if I deny your request."

"It is not a request, dear brother," she said sweetly, "but a command. I shall be miserable if we are anywhere but London for Christmas. I shall be a social outcast, and you would not wish that for your darling sister, now would you?"

"Certainly not," he sighed.

Elizabeth hid her smile behind her teacup, and I pitied Charles all the more. He needed a wife who would support him in his love for the countryside. If Charles had his way, he would never leave Pemberley. London did not suit him as much as it suited his sisters.

I would not be surprised if he purchased his own country estate very soon. He had spoken of it often enough...

I sighed, my eyes falling on the beautiful woman seated across from Mr. Bingley's sisters.

Perhaps Charles could be encouraged to find a country house if he had some reason to leave London. It would not take much.

~

*M*iss Jane Bennet's arrival at Pemberley was met with equal measures of skepticism and excitement. Elizabeth was, of course, thrilled to welcome her sister to Derbyshire, and Charles seemed to have taken an interest in the young woman even before she arrived.

Caroline and Louisa, predictably, were irritated with the mere notion that another young woman was coming to Pemberley.

Caroline saw everything as competition, whether it was for my attention or the attention of anyone else in the house. That woman would never be satisfied. I pitied the man who might one day make her a wife.

It would not be me.

Jane Bennet was just as lovely as her sister, though the two of them could not have been more different in temperament.

Where Elizabeth was bright and quick to laugh, Jane was more reserved and seemed to prefer to watch and observe than to participate. Elizabeth's dark hair curled playfully around her ears and across her forehead, while Jane's fair hair was straight and well-kept and never escaped from her fastidious coiffure.

Clearly the elder in her demeanor, Jane Bennet was also a sweet young lady with a smile for everyone, and she did not seem to notice how vicious Caroline or Louisa were trying to be in their conversation.

A brilliant tactic, perhaps? Or was she simply too sweet to notice. I resolved to ask that question of Elizabeth when I was able to speak with her, but now that her sister was at Pemberley, the inevitability of her departure loomed over me.

Had I squandered my opportunity to speak to her in private?

~

Only two nights after Jane Bennet's arrival, I was certain that Mr. Bingley was on the verge of proposing to the young woman. She had very clearly captivated him, and she, in turn, seemed very fond of his excitable antics.

They were an odd pairing, but one that seemed so natural as to prevent me from finding any opposition to it. Though her background was the same as Elizabeth's, and I wondered if I should say something to Charles to that effect.

Would marriage to a young lady of no fortune or prospects ruin his reputation? It would do nothing but improve hers...

But when I thought of Miss Elizabeth Bennet, and the way her fine eyes sparkled in the candlelit room, I could not imagine having affection for any other young lady.

My aunt was determined that I would marry her daughter--But Anne deBourgh was a depressing figure of a young lady. Sickly, and without many opinions that were not a pale version of her mother's.

But Elizabeth Bennet? Her laughter was addictive and her presence was a balm that I had not expected. She was, however, infuriating, and we had argued over many subjects contained in my precious books. Books that I had not expected she had ever read.

She was a constant source of surprise.

But, did I love her?

Marriage should be about love, should it not? But I wondered if I was truly capable of the emotion.

I'd had little opportunity to experience it, and the last time I had come close I had been no more than a boy, and the young woman in question had been engaged to another man.

But my guest would be leaving in two days. I would not allow myself to make a mistake that could put my own happiness in jeopardy. Nor would I fall under the spell of an unworthy woman who sought only to better her own situation.

I could not allow myself to be fooled. I must be strong.

$\mathcal{I}$ had been in the library for some time when I heard the softest of knocks on the door.

"Yes?"

"Mr. Darcy, may I enter?"

I nodded, and she stepped inside. I looked up from the book I was pretending to read. "Miss Bennet, this is a surprise."

"I had hoped to find you here, Mr. Darcy," she said. "You have been absent from our company for the last two nights and I did wonder if I had done something to offend you."

I was instantly ashamed of my selfish actions. For she had, truly, done nothing wrong... she was only herself, and it was my fault that I could not bring myself to overlook who she was.

"No, indeed," I said. "I have merely been taken up with the affairs of the estate. Pemberley requires a steady hand to keep its ledgers in order."

"I do not doubt it," she said. "My own father stays up late

many nights poring over his own ledgers, but I suspect that his worries are not so great as yours."

A silence fell between us and I turned a page in my book, hoping that she would take some sign of my disinterest and leave. But she stepped farther into the room.

"Perhaps you would like to take the air," she said. "A walk through the gardens before supper, perhaps?"

"Now?"

"I thought it might be nice," she said. "The sunset is beautiful over the lake, and--"

She paused. "And Jane and I will depart for Hertfordshire in the morning."

Ah, yes, that.

I had been dreading it almost as much as I had wished for that day to come.

"I do not wish to impose..." she said.

"Of course not," I said hastily, rising to my feet.

"But if you would like to walk with me, I would welcome your company."

I could not bring myself to refuse.

We walked through the gardens and fell into a companionable silence. I found it soothing; her presence was calming, and she held herself with a poise that made me doubt myself all over again.

The gardens were on the south side of the house, the rose bushes hugged low stone walls and ivy crept over the edge of the house.

She paused in her walk, and pulled a flower from a nearby bush and twirled it between her fingers as she studied the sunset.

It was a picture of perfection: the warm light on her skin,

the look of wonder on her face, the gentle breeze that tugged at the curls that framed her face...

She looked like a woman in a mythological painting.

"I will never forget my time here," she said softly. "Or your kindness. I have spent far too much time thinking about what might have happened to me if you had not pulled me from the forest..."

"We shall not speak of such things," I said. "You are safe and well, and your injuries have healed."

"Not all of them," she said ruefully. She held up her hand, the perfection of her skin was marred by the wound she had obtained in her fall from the saddle as it caught on one of the sharp metal buckles.

"I shall be fortunate to find a husband who can bear to look upon such a flaw," she said ruefully.

Before I could stop myself, I took hold of her hand, drew it to my lips, and pressed a kiss against her knuckles, close to the edge of the bandage.

Her skin was delicate and soft and smelled of the perfumed flower she had plucked.

"It is but a small flaw," I said. "I would have a severe judgement of any man who would be distressed by such a thing."

She looked at me, her mouth parting almost imperceptibly. For a moment, I thought she might pull her hand away, that I had overstepped my bounds, but she only looked at me without pulling away or saying anything.

I knew what I was doing, and I knew I should stop, but I couldn't. I knew that I was doing wrong, but I couldn't let it go. Not when she was looking at me in that way, her lips slightly parted, her eyes wide...

I raised my hand to her cheek, cupping it gently. She responded, leaning into my hand and closing her eyes.

My body acted without my direction, and my arms pulled her against me. I lowered my head to hers, and she met me halfway, tilting her chin up so her lips could meet mine.

It was a terrible, terrible thing to do, but I was lost in the kiss.

I was the one to draw away, for I knew it was wrong. She stepped back, but only a little.

"I must apologize," I said. "I did not--"

"No," she said quickly. "It was my choice. I know my own mind and I--"

"Miss Bennet, I would not--"

"Mr. Darcy, am I a fool to hope that you might have some affection for me?"

Damn everything. I did. From the moment I'd held her in my arms on that stormy afternoon I knew that I was bound for trouble.

"Miss Bennet, you have been my guest here at Pemberley. I would not take advantage of you or put your reputation at risk... Whatever affection I might have for you, it ends tonight. You will be leaving Pemberley in the morning, and I-- I must apologize. I do not know what came over me."

She stepped back, her expression stricken.

"I see."

"You must understand that we cannot-- I cannot... You are not--"

"I understand very well," she said. "I have heard Miss Bingley speak about it at length. You must marry a suitable young woman, of course. How could I have ever thought--"

Without another word, Elizabeth turned and ran for the house.

"Miss Bennet," I called after her.

But she did not stop.

"Miss Bennet!"

My voice was raised in the quiet of the night and the servants would be sure to hear.

"Elizabeth!"

It was no use. She was gone.

6

ELIZABETH

*M*y lips burned as hotly as my cheeks as I ran for the safety of the house. I could hear him calling for me.

Calling my name from the garden, and my heart tore into pieces to hear it.

He did not love me.

No, that was not the worst of it.

He could not bring himself to love me because of who my family was.

I would never be able to explain anything of it to Jane. Poor Jane.

In the few days she had been at Pemberley, she had developed a deep affection for Mr. Charles Bingley. I could not blame her, of course, he was everything she might have wanted in a gentleman. And nothing that could be found in the gentlemen and officers who populated Hertfordshire.

As much as we had spoken of my own struggle to find the very deepest love, and my requirements for a husband, what Jane had wanted had never *really* been discussed.

She had wanted a kind man, of course. One of learning and some reading... no gamblers, of course, and someone who could make her laugh and forget her troubles. Handsome, witty, charming, those were all expected.

If that gentleman could be Charles Bingley, I would never argue with her choice. He was delightful, but his sisters... his sisters were a nightmare that I would not have been able to manage.

But Jane seemed to take everything that Caroline and Louisa said in stride, and I wondered if she was just ignoring the poison that flowed from Caroline's cherry lips, or that she truly did not find it insulting or offensive.

I hoped for Jane's sake that it was the former and not the latter.

She was nothing like those women, and it pained me to see her keeping company with snakes.

I rushed into the house and ran up the stairs to the bedchamber I had been given. The Rose Room. I had not even asked why it was called that... or why he had chosen it for me.

Yesterday I might have cared.

Tonight, it meant nothing.

I ran to it, threw open the door, and slammed it shut behind me. I locked it and leaned back against the door, desperate for a moment of quiet. No thoughts of his cruel words, or Caroline's bitter judgements.

No, not even of Jane's unexpected happiness.

Just a moment where I could calm myself and replace those thoughts with something else... anything else. I breathed slowly until I could feel the rage, the pain, and the sadness, slowly recede.

I could see my reflection in the vanity mirror. My cheeks

were pink and my eyes were bright with unshed tears. I would not cry for him, or for whatever I thought I might have wanted...

I rubbed the back of my uninjured hand across my lips to wipe away the memory of his kiss. *How dare he.*

The bed had been re-made and turned down, and I contemplated just lying down and giving myself up to slumber and make the morning of our departure come all the faster.

Instead I settled for changing into my nightgown and climbing into bed with a book I had taken from Mr. Darcy's library.

A gentle knock on the door startled me from my reading, and Jane entered the room.

"Lizzy, are you not coming to supper?"

I shook my head. "No, I do not feel well at all."

"But it is our last night at Pemberley," she said. "Are you not sad to be leaving?"

"No," I replied. "I do not think I am. I might have been this morning, or perhaps even yesterday. But tonight I am not sad at all. I am looking forward to returning to Longbourn, out mother will have been a mess without us there to assist her."

"I have no doubt of that," Jane said ruefully. "We have both missed the Regimental Ball, and I do not think she will forgive us very soon."

"She might if you return with an engagement," I said and forced myself to smile. If I could find no happiness here, perhaps Jane could.

My sister's cheeks flushed pink. "Do you really believe he might? It has not been very long at all, and Miss Bingley speaks ceaselessly of Miss Darcy and how accomplished and lovely she is. Do you think that she would prefer if Mr. Bingley married Mr. Darcy's sister instead?"

I closed my book and regarded my sister carefully. "I have not met Miss Darcy," I said. "And from what I have heard of her, she is, indeed, a lovely an accomplished young woman. But she is very young... far too young for a gentleman such as Mr. Bingley. As much as Caroline might wish to have her family tied to Mr. Darcy's, this is not how it will happen."

Jane sighed happily. "I do hope that you are right. Are you certain that you will not come down to supper?"

I shook my head. "You will have to make my apologies."

"Will you tell me what is the matter?"

"Perhaps tomorrow," I said with a small smile.

Jane left me alone then, and I tried my best to sleep, but even though my eyelids grew heavy, I watched the candle on the bedside table until it burned down to nothing and snuffed itself on the melted wax.

I could not stop my need to think of what might have been, what I had hoped for in my heart, and what was now gone.

~

I woke with a start to the rattle of a carriage and the sound of hooves on the gravel.

I sat up in bed, my heart pounding.

It was morning.

The new day, and our journey back to Longbourn, was upon us.

I threw off the blanket and sat up in bed as I tried to collect my thoughts. I needed to dress quickly and sneak out of the house with Jane before anyone else in the house saw us. They would have said their goodbyes at the supper table, and would not force themselves out of bed to wave to our departing carriage.

I would not regret any of it. I refused to spend one moment more in Caroline Bingley's company than was absolutely necessary, and the less I saw of Mr. Fitzwilliam Darcy, the better.

Jane had, thoughtfully, brought my trunk from Silverwood, and reluctantly laid aside Georgiana Darcy's beautiful gowns in favor of my own worn muslin with velvet ribbon roses at the bodice that we had made last winter.

I dressed quickly, pulling on my gown and my boots, and hurried out of the room.

I was not surprised to find the house quiet. Mr. Bingley and his sisters were, indeed, still in their own chambers. I could only guess that they had drunk too much the night before and were sleeping off their excess.

I did not know if they were the sort to drink too much, but Caroline had been desperate to get Mr. Darcy to drink more than a glass of wine since the moment I had arrived, and I wondered if she had finally succeeded.

Although I doubted that even a drunk Fitzwilliam Darcy would be an agreeable sort of gentleman. Perhaps I had finally seen the arrogance that Caroline had mentioned so often in our conversations.

Jane and I could sneak out, and no one would be the wiser.

The house was silent and still, the only sound was the crackling of the fire in the sitting room on the main floor.

I waited until I saw Jane's head peek around the corner, and I hurried to join her.

Our trunks were waiting in the courtyard and the

footmen worked to secure them to the roof. Mrs. Reynolds was, of course, there to see us safely on our way, and I embraced the older woman tightly and murmured my thanks for all of her care.

"I do hope that you will find your way back to Pemberley," she said. "You are welcome any time. I will tell Miss Georgiana all about you. I do believe that you would have been the very best of friends."

I wondered if there might have been something else on the housekeeper's mind, but she did not say anything more.

"I hope that I may come back this way again very soon," I said, though I did not know if I could bear to look upon this part of the country ever again.

Jane hugged Mrs. Reynolds as well, and we climbed into the carriage. The footmen closed the door and the carriage lurched into motion. I waved to Mrs. Reynolds through the window and watched the house, halfway hoping that I might see a familiar figure, tall and aloof, in the window... but I saw nothing but the reflection of the colors of the dawn in the high windows.

The carriage progressed up the hill, past the lake with black swans upon its glassy surface, and onward beyond the sycamore groves toward Lambton. We would stop at Silverwood to see the Darrows, and then be on our way to London. And then, home.

~

*J*ane and I chatted easily about our time at Pemberley as the carriage rocked along, and I tried not to think of Mr. Darcy, or how his words in the garden had made me feel.

Instead, I focused on my sister, and how happy she seemed to be.

How could I be sad when she was so happy?

"Charles promised that he would come to Hertfordshire," she said. "Do you think he will?"

"I do hope so," I replied, though I was not certain that such a thing would be possible. What if Mr. Darcy had made it his mission to dissuade his friend from offering any suit to Jane as well?

If our family was not good enough for *him*, how could it be good enough for Mr. Bingley?

I shook my head and tried to banish such thoughts from my mind. A gentleman had his pride, and he must know his own mind.

I had had my say, as I knew I should, and it was no longer my place to interfere in the matter. I recognized that.

But I did not have to like it.

We reached Silverwood, and the household was all abuzz with our arrival. Mrs. Darrow had heard of our time at Pemberley from Claudia, and she was more than eager to hear all that Mrs. Reynolds had to say.

We spent the afternoon at the Darrows' house and were invited to stay on for supper, but I could not shake my restlessness.

Thankfully, Jane had sensed my desire to press on in our journey, and we made our apologies before setting away again with fresh horses and a hamper of food for the journey.

I had never been so eager to return to Longbourn, but now it was putting distance between myself and Mr. Darcy; that was my main concern.

7

DARCY

*E*lizabeth had not come to supper, but I did not venture into the dining room until I was certain that she was not there. Jane Bennet was pleasant company, to be sure, but her smiles and attention were focused upon Charles, who seemed more like a smitten lad than a gentleman of five thousand a year.

Caroline and Louisa were as sour as ever, and Caroline seemed determined to force me to drink more than two glasses of wine with my supper. I did not overindulge at meals, or any time for that matter, but there was something about how I felt that evening that made it difficult to refuse.

The dining room was a little emptier without Elizabeth Bennet's bright presence and her infectious laughter—the witty banter and teasing remarks were lacking, leaving only Caroline's bitterness and Louisa's haughty silences behind.

When Jane took her leave of the party, there was, at once, a discussion of the Bennet sisters and I could scarcely hide my disdain for it all.

Caroline, of course, noticed my disquiet.

"I suppose he had enough of Miss Elizabeth at last," Caroline observed archly. "She has a talent for inspiring strong emotions in her admirers, but she can leave them quite uncomfortable, too."

"Why do you suppose he is in love with her, if she makes him so uncomfortable?" Louisa asked.

Caroline gasped dramatically. "In love with her, Louisa you cannot be serious! Mr. Darcy loves nothing so much as this house and his dear sister. I cannot imagine that he would love a country mouse like Eliza Bennet!"

My grip tightened on the arm of my chair as I fought the urge to argue. How dare they speak in such a way--

"She is very plain, is she not," Louisa said with a satisfied smile. It was a hideous expression on her cold, dull face.

"I must agree," Caroline said. "if it were not for those fine eyes, she would be too plain to remark upon. But she is too bold in her way of speaking, and she does not know her place in society... A proper young lady would know how to behave around her betters."

"Her eyes *are* very pretty," Louisa added, as if she were describing a horse.

"Too pretty," Caroline laughed. "Can you believe that Mr. Darcy might have been foolish enough to consider asking for her hand?"

"Surely not," Louisa cried. "Mr. Darcy you must repudiate this at once!"

It was difficult to keep the anger from my voice and I did not know if I would be able to control myself if I did speak.

It was not a question of my feelings, but I *had* been foolish. I had allowed myself to believe that I could control my emotions, and that, perhaps, society and her place in it did not matter... But that was a lie. It would always matter.

I had been raised to believe certain things about marriage, and about the woman that I would fall in love with. But as the years had passed and the thought of ever finding love had diminished, I thought instead of what sort of woman would be best for Pemberley.

Elizabeth Bennet was as different from his Georgiana as could be imagined. She was wilful, proud, opinionated... changeable. Infuriating.

She was everything he wanted in a partner.

"I have listened to you harpies long enough," I snarled.

I stood, pushing back my chair and nearly knocking over my untouched wine glass. I stalked out of the room, feeling the hateful glances of Caroline Bingley and Louisa Hurst follow me out of the room.

"Where is he going?" Caroline asked, confused.

"I am not sure," Louisa said.

I didn't look back. I didn't have to.

~

I paced back and forth in my chambers, trying to distract myself from my anger.

I thought of Elizabeth and her smile, her laughter.

It was only with her, in those brief moments where we could be alone that I felt I could truly be myself. Walking in the gardens, visiting the stables...

I had not asked her if she felt brave enough to ride again, but I had wanted to. I had wanted to be there for that moment when she discovered that she could trust the horse to look after her.

But worst of all, I could not keep my feelings from her.

I wanted to be with her, to watch her smile and tease, to

listen to her speak of all manner of nonsense, to hear her read poetry as we sat in the evening, sharing a glass of wine.

How had I allowed myself to fall in love with her?

It was almost a relief when I heard Charles Bingley's voice in the hall outside my chambers.

I would need an excuse for my outburst and I would need to be prepared for his questions.

"Darcy," he called through the door.

I had not realized that I had been pacing so quickly that I had exhausted myself. I inhaled deeply, then exhaled slowly, trying to regain my composure.

"Come in," I said as I turned to look at him.

He opened the door and entered the room. Charles could always be counted upon to make rash decisions... He led with the heart, not with the head. He was the one who came to me for rational advice... but perhaps it was time that I asked him for some impractical advice.

I was never so impulsive that I was unable to choose the right course, but I wondered if this time, I had not fallen victim to my own weakness for reason and rational thought.

Elizabeth wasn't an irrational creature, and my admiration for her felt just as wild and unfamiliar.

"I think I have been a fool," I began, then paused, trying to find the words.

Charles walked across the room and poured himself a glass of brandy before sitting down opposite me. "I am always happy to listen, Darcy. You should know that by now."

"You have asked me many times to describe my ideal wife. The woman who would be mistress of this estate," I began. "I told you that I wanted a woman who was as intelligent and wise as she was beautiful."

"You are describing Miss Elizabeth Bennet," Charles said with a smile. "She is very beautiful."

"I fear that I have made a mockery of everything I thought I wanted," I said. I looked into my glass, watching the amber liquid swirl. "I know that I am not perfect, and I have made many mistakes--"

"I will stop you there, Darcy," Charles said. "Now, you must be truthful with me."

I met his steady gaze. "Am I not always truthful with you?"

"When it comes to matters of the heart, I do not believe that you are," Charles said.

I chuckled and accepted the glass of bourbon he held out to me.

"When did you grow so wise?" I asked.

Charles smiled. "Forgive me, Darcy. I will speak plainly."

I nodded, bracing myself for the blow that was sure to come.

"It is not Elizabeth's loveliness alone that has caught your eye," Charles said. "I have known you long enough to know that you are not the sort of man to be so easily swayed. But there is something more to your admiration, is there not? Something that goes beyond the physical?"

I opened my mouth to speak, but closed it again. I knew that I could not say that I loved her. That I would have chosen her over all the ladies of my acquaintance. That I could not endure days without her smile. All of it was ridiculous.

"You do not have to say anything," Charles said. "Your silence speaks volumes. I only ask that you take your time with this. There is a reason that you have been so particular."

"I am very aware of the different circles that exist within the bounds of our English society," I said. "I am well aware of my duty to marry a lady of a suitable background and breeding."

"Yes," Charles said. "But I am not referring to the rules of society." He raised his hand when I opened my mouth to protest. "I am not lecturing," he said. "I know very well that you choose your friends with care, and you are always mindful of your duty... But there is something to be said for the strength of your feelings, and for the love that exists between the two of you. I have seen it, even in the short time that you have known her, there is, indeed, something there. Something powerful."

I shook my head, my heart heavy with doubt.

"I cannot say that I am not tempted at the idea of it," I said. "But it is too risky. I have enough to contend with."

"I know it is not my place to say this, Darcy," Charles began. "But I do not think that you have given yourself enough credit. I think the idea of loving someone is equally as frightening as the idea of losing someone. Have you done something to endanger this chance at happiness?"

I was silent, thinking. The alcohol had taken hold and I felt a warmth spread through my limbs as I thought about what Charles had said. I swallowed the rest of my glass, and then stood and walked to the table where I poured myself another.

"Another?" Charles asked, watching me with a knowing smile.

I shook my head. "Would you think me a fool if I said that I had thrown that all aside for something as simple as pride?"

Charles looked at me strangely. "Pride? And how would you do that?"

"I... Perhaps it was not pride at all. Perhaps it was something more hurtful. I-- I told Elizabeth that I could not love her. That I should not... that I should know better because of our stations in life."

"What?"

Charles stared at me and I could feel heat spreading across the back of my neck.

Embarrassment. Shame. Guilt.

"You told her that you couldn't love her because of-- money? Darcy! I am aghast!"

"And you," I cried. "What of your affection for her elder sister? Are you not worried about the same possibility? That she is pretending her affection to gain your fortune? That she is a fortune hunter with a grasping mother who will thrust not one, but three more unmarried daughters at your circle of friends in the hope that another well-moneyed gentleman will take an interest in one of them?"

My face was hot and I knew that I was shouting. But Charles' expression was impassive.

"I never given it a moment's thought," Charles said simply. "I have a duty to my family just as you do. I do not have an estate like Pemberley to think of, but I am building toward it. Someone like Jane Bennet might be the very best person to do that with. I do not need a high-born lady who can do nothing more useful than play the piano and talk about the weather... I want a partner. Someone I can talk with about everything and nothing until the moon sinks below the horizon and the sun rises once more. That is what matters more than society, and you would do well to remember it."

The words resonated in my mind. He was right.

In my short-sightedness and pride, I had hurt Elizabeth with my words, and I had meant to do it.

Charles shook his head. "I have never known you to be so much a fool about a woman. Lady Catherine will oppose you until the end of her days, but that might not be a terrible position to be in. You will inherit Rosings Park before long, and I would much rather be tied to a young woman who makes me laugh than one who cannot be bothered to speak to me for the duration of our union."

Without a backward glance, Charles took his bourbon and walked out of the room. I paced in front of the fireplace until I could not rationalize any longer.

I needed to find a way I could repair things with Elizabeth. And hope that it was not too late.

8

ELIZABETH

I had still not told Jane about Mr. Darcy's cruel rejection. It was my fervent wish that he had not passed his prejudice on to his friend—Jane had received only one letter from Caroline Bingley since our return to Hertfordshire, and though it had begun with the words "*my dear friend*" it had been a cold and unfriendly letter that had left me feeling angry and frustrated while Jane had tried to explain away the meaning behind the words that had not been said...

How long would Jane wait for Mr. Bingley to visit? Would he visit at all? Was that too much to hope for?

If it was, I wanted to tell Jane before she admitted that she loved Mr. Bingley and she was waiting for him to return so she could tell him so.

He would never come to Hertfordshire. I knew it already. But I could never speak those thoughts aloud. Especially not to Jane. I didn't want to make them true.

I couldn't bear the thought of our sisters watching both Jane and I succumbing to the weight of disappointment and unhappiness. Kitty and Lydia would marry first, of that I was certain. They would, each of them, find a handsome officer to sweep them away to an adventurous new life away from Hertfordshire, and I would only be able to wish for the days when they were as they were now--arguing over who would wear which bonnet to Meryton, or who was going to eat the last tart from their afternoon tea.

Most of all, I wished that I could believe that I would never be disappointed again, that a gentleman would disregard everything about me except for myself... I had thought Mr. Darcy could do that. That my station would mean nothing to him. But I was wrong, and he was just as arrogant and snobbish as Caroline had said.

The most disagreeable gentleman of my unfortunate acquaintance.

Perhaps I would be perfectly happy alone.

Perhaps marriage did not matter. I knew several women who were well past marrying and childbearing age who were very happy, indeed. They lived alone or with family members, raising chickens or sheep, writing letters, visiting museums... and doing as they pleased without anyone to say no. Well, within reason, of course.

But they were happy. At least, they seemed to be.

Perhaps I could learn to be so, too.

~

It felt like a lifetime had passed since Jane and I had been at Pemberley. We had missed the Regimental Ball, but it did not feel as though anything of any importance had occurred.

Lady Lucas supplied our mother with every piece of

gossip worth knowing, but even she had had nothing to say for far too long.

We were invited to tea at Lucas Lodge, however, in the weeks leading up to the Christmas Assembly.

Seated at the card tables, I tried my best to feign an interest in Lady Lucas' conversation, but she seemed overly interested in a new family who had just moved into an estate that had long been unoccupied.

"I have not learned their names as yet," Lady Lucas said, "but they have been in Meryton for only a month and there's already a great deal of talk about them--but perhaps you already know them, Miss Elizabeth?"

Surprised by Lady Lucas' sudden attention, I shook my head. "How should I know them?" I replied. "I have had no call to be acquainted with anyone new to town."

"They have a house in London since the gentleman has a good income, his two sisters are with him, and two other gentlemen. I do hope that they are not all spoken for. Hertfordshire is severely lacking in eligible gentlemen who are not dressed in Regimental red, do you not agree?"

I wasn't certain if she was talking to me, or to the entire table, and I did not reply. The other ladies around us laughed and twittered over the possibility of a new gentleman in town, but I was worried for another reason.

"Do you know anything else about them?" I asked.

Lady Lucas looked thoughtful. "Well, as I have heard it, the gentleman's family has been in London for some time. They are a fashionable, handsome group, and the ladies are very elegant."

I raised an eyebrow and hoped that it would be enough to signal my lack of interest, but I wondered perhaps if the

family was one that I would recognize if I saw them in the
street.

"Do you not know their names," my mother demanded. "It
is most difficult to guess at who to speak to if we do not know
their name! And where are they staying?"

"Ah, yes," Lady Lucas exclaimed, "I have remembered
now."

I did not believe that she had ever forgotten, she was
simply waiting for more attention to be brought to her words.

"He has leased Netherfield Park," she said loudly enough
that everyone in the drawing room could hear her.
Appreciative noises filled the room as the other ladies began
to talk amongst themselves. Netherfield Park was a grand
estate that was almost as fine as Pemberley... Expansive
grounds and forests filled with beautiful deer and pheasants-
-enviable hunting for any sportsman. The house was
beautiful and large, if a bit out of date. It was certainly in
need of some care, but whoever leased the property would
be expected to improve upon it within a short amount of
time.

"Mr. Charles Bingley," Lady Lucas said. "That is his name."

"Oh! Jane," my mother cried. She gripped Jane's arm and I
fought the urge to run from the room as my sister took hold
of my hand.

"He has come, Lizzy," she hissed in my ear. "It is as I had
hoped!"

"It has been months," I whispered back and winced as she
squeezed my hand tighter.

"He has not forgotten me," Jane said firmly. "It is as I knew
it would be. Caroline has spoken to him and made him
remember his promises."

"Indeed," I whispered. "I do hope that it may be so."

Lady Lucas cleared her throat and directed a pointed glare at us. Jane smiled and I forced myself to do the same.

"I have already sent Sir William to Netherfield Park to make our introductions," she said loftily. "And also to be certain that he will remember to consider our Charlotte as a partner at the Christmas Assembly."

"Of course," my mother murmured, though I could see from the expression on her face that she wished that she could shout at Mr. Bennet at once to demand that he do the very same thing.

My father would resist, of course, even though Jane's happiness might depend upon it. He was a stubborn man, but perhaps he would see fit to give his eldest daughter such a simple chance at happiness.

There could be no other reason for Mr. Bingley to be here, and no other reason to bring his sisters and Mr. Hurst with them. But the second gentleman... Who could that be?

Surely, it could not be Mr. Darcy.

He wouldn't dare...

∼

*O*ur return to Longbourn was taken in haste, and as our mother swept into the house, she began to shout for our father immediately.

Jane and I retired to the parlor and I did my best to calm Jane's nerves.

"But it is he, Lizzy. He has come all the way to Hertfordshire *and* leased one of the finest estates in the countryside. You cannot deny that this is... this is everything I have hoped for."

"I hope that it is," I said. "But we cannot be certain that it is

Mr. Bingley until we know more than what Lady Lucas has to say. She has mistaken people before!"

Jane nodded and bit her lip. "The Christmas Assembly is not far away, I am certain that I shall see him there. I am sure that he will dance with me."

I forced a smile. "I wonder what conversations happened to make him decide to come here after so long without any word?"

"We shall not speak of such things," Jane said. "I wish only to be happy that he is here. Can you not give me that?"

I let out heavy sigh. "I suppose."

There was a crash from the floor above our heads and Jane groaned and ran upstairs to see what commotion was happening between Lydia and Kitty.

Another argument, no doubt.

I did not want to remain in the parlor for too long, there was far too much chance that my mother would return and demand some errand of me. I could hear her arguing with my father in his study. I knew already that he did not wish to leave the house--the almanac had predicted snow, which would have been lovely for the Christmas Assembly, but terrible for a social call on a new neighbor. Especially a forced one.

I pulled a shawl around my shoulders and slipped out of the house into the gardens. I did my best to appreciate the crisp air and the whisper of white flakes that were beginning to fall from the darkening sky.

My father's almanac was never wrong. That was one thing I could always count on.

There was no way to know how much show might fall, but I was relieved that my father would not be sent out into it to make our case with Mr. Bingley. It was enough that Mr.

Darcy had already made an assumption as to what sort of family we were...

I walked for some time, allowing the cold to chill my bones and soothe my nerves.

I could not help but think of Mr. Bingley, and of the gentleman that was with him.

Mr. Darcy.

What was he doing in Hertfordshire? I wondered.

Why had he come?

If Mr. Bingley had come to see Jane--if he had come to renew his affections and make an offer of marriage then all of Jane's desperate dreams would come true.

But what of mine?

~

Over supper, Papa had, once more defied our mother's demands for him to visit Netherfield Park.

"Why must you vex me so, Mr. Bennet?" she cried. "My poor nerves will not survive this Christmas if I am to be kept in suspense for all this time! Every other household in Hertfordshire will have visited Netherfield Park by now and will have made a great commotion about *their* unmarried daughters, but you cannot summon the energy to do so even though your eldest daughter is the only one deserving of his attentions! Mr. Bennet!"

My father's stoic temperament was in equal ways comforting and infuriating. I knew that he took special delight in tormenting our mother, and this particular event seemed to be no exception.

"My dear, Mrs. Bennet," he began when she had stopped shrieking. "I cannot go to Netherfield Park."

"But *why,* Mr. Bennet," she cried. "Why do you forsake us in such a way? Do you not have any care for our position in this society? My dear Jane, poor Jane. I am sorry that your father cares nothing for your future--"

"Mama, please," I sighed. "You are overwrought."

"I cannot go to Netherfield Park, Madam," my father continued. "Because I have already been. Before Sir William, might I add."

Mrs. Bennet's mouth dropped open and her false tears ceased to dampen her cheeks.

"What?"

"Indeed," Mr. Bennet said primly. "It was Mr. Bingley himself who stopped me in Meryton to ask for directions to Longbourn. Happily, I was able to bring him directly to the house."

"Here," Mrs. Bennet cried. "I was--"

"Unfortunately, not at home," Mr. Bennet replied. "The day of Lady Lucas' tea, I believe."

"Oh, Mr. Bennet," my mother cried as she launched herself at her husband. My father laughed as she wrapped her arms around his neck and kissed him soundly on the cheek.

"Perhaps we shall be saved from embarrassment after all," she sighed.

Jane could not have looked happier, but I could not fight the ache in my belly as I thought of Fitzwilliam Darcy.

I could not bear to speak to him, but perhaps he would feel the same and would avoid my company as well.

The approach of the Christmas Assembly might make any attempt at such a thing impossible, but I could hold on to a slight hope... it was all I had left.

9

ELIZABETH

The Meryton assembly rooms were not the easiest to decorate, but when the Christmas Assembly was near, the ladies who took charge of such things made certain that everything was as grand as could be managed.

Lady Lucas was always in command of the decor, and despite the snow there had been several deliveries from London of festive bouquets, bushels of gold-painted apples, and cartloads of fresh cut pine boughs from the forest nearby.

The hall was decorated with all the richness of the season, and the overwhelming scents of holly, pine, and beeswax would fill the air. I had even seen a few sprigs of mistletoe hung in strategic places around the hall, and I dreaded being caught beneath it.

The long tables were heavy with food and bowls of cider and rum punch.

Every year the dinner that accompanied the Christmas Assembly grew more and more elaborate, and this year was no exception.

The smell of roasted turkey, oyster stuffing, and gingerbread permeated the hall as the servants brought in the savory hot dishes in large covered platters. There was a thick cream sauce for the boiled potatoes and mashed turnips, and an array of hard cheeses, trifle, and artful marzipan fruit for dessert.

The Christmas Assembly was the only event to which our family was able to arrive early... even Lydia, who could never be hurried to do anything, took every pain to be certain that she was dressed and ready to leave at the correct time.

Everyone in Hertfordshire was in agreement that the Christmas Assembly was the most enjoyable social event of the entire year.

Although it was tempting to fill my plate with food and drink far too much rum punch, I knew that I had to be careful not to overwhelm myself. There was nothing worse than not being able to dance once the musicians took their places.

Beside me, Jane was still nibbling on a slice of gingerbread.

"Have you seen him yet?" I whispered.

Jane shook her head. Since our father's announcement of his meeting with Mr. Bingley, Jane had waited every day for the gentleman to come to Longbourn.

Or for an invitation to come for her to come to tea... but nothing ever arrived, and neither did he.

How could he make her wait in such a manner?

Jane was one of the most sought after marriage prospects in all of Hertfordshire, and this meant that she likely would not remain on the marriage market for long. That is, when she decided to turn her eye from Netherfield Park and the distant possibility that Mr. Bingley presented.

"He will come tonight, Lizzy," she said. "Do you not think so?"

I nodded and smiled. "Of course he will. After all, Mr. Bingley is a man of his word. He will not refuse to come simply because of a little snow."

Although, Caroline Bingley might. I wondered how much power she held over her younger brother--was it enough to keep him from Jane's side when he was so close?

Jane smiled at my reassurance and I thought she looked much more at ease with herself.

She was beautiful as ever, and I couldn't help but admire how well her golden hair looked when it was so perfectly coiled and braided with and set with a garland of tiny white flowers that I had chosen from our mother's ornament box.

There was something different in her blue eyes as she spoke about Mr. Bingley.

"He will be here," she replied firmly. "That is the only thing that I am certain of."

I patted her hand reassuringly as more guests arrived and the musicians began to make their way to the dance floor.

"There is still time," I said.

Jane's smile did not falter. "I know."

$\sim$

I did wish that I believed that Mr. Bingley would come, but after the food had been cleared away and the banquet tables were moved to make space for the dancers, I began to doubt it.

In the corner of the large hall, Lydia was already on her third dance partner, and although I had asked her to be cautious with her ballroom activity, I was too busy to play the part of chaperone to her at the moment.

I smiled as I watched her flit around the floor with her string of admirers, for once not putting anyone in fear for their health or their toes.

And then, finally, I saw him. Mr. Bingley's curling golden hair stood out in the crowd, and I watched him as he spoke to Colonel Forster who stood as near to the rum punch as he could manage without attracting too much attention.

I searched the room for Jane, and found her on the dance floor on the arm of a slender young officer who looked as though he would make a better partner for Kitty than Jane as they would be closer in age.

But I did not see Mr. Darcy.

I was fully engaged with my own thoughts and didn't notice when Mr. Bingley came to stand beside me.

"Miss Elizabeth Bennet?" He smiled."Are you free for the next dance?"

"Oh!" I jumped. "Mr. Bingley! Of course!"

The gentleman bowed. "If you would be so kind as to take my arm?"

"Indeed, I shall!"

I did not hesitate to place my hand through his elbow and dance away with him. "There is my sister," I said, motioning toward Jane. "She was looking for you."

Mr. Bingley smiled as he looked in her direction. "She looks very beautiful this evening," he said. "I do hope that I have not missed the opportunity to put my name on her dance card?"

"I am certain that as soon as she knows you are here that it will be quite empty of other names." I said, smiling back.

"Miss Bennet, might I ask you something?"

"Of course."

"If you were to think of Pemberley, what are the first things that come to your mind?"

It was my turn to start. "I am not sure what you mean, Mr. Bingley."

But as soon as I said the words, I knew what I should say.

"It is a very grand estate," I began. "One that I am not certain would be agreeable to someone like me."

"Would you be happy in a house so large?"

I laughed. "By myself? Certainly not."

"And if you were not alone?"

"Then I should have to be there with someone who was agreeable to be with--someone I could talk to, someone who would fill the empty spaces with laughter and life... I could not live in a place that was empty of such things."

I regarded him carefully.

"And why would you ask me something like that?"

Mr. Bingley's smile was disarming. "I was curious as to whether your answer would be the same as someone else that I know very well. And it happens that it is... very similar, indeed."

"I see."

"I notice that you have not asked where Mr. Darcy is this evening."

"I have not," I said.

"He angered you when you last spoke, did he not?"

"I--" I paused briefly as the tempo of the music slowed to allow the dancers to twirl in place. "He did," I said firmly.

"Would you forgive him for the insult he gave you?"

I froze in place, and then remembered my steps. "You... He told you?"

Mr. Bingley inclined his head. "He did."

"And-- Did you agree with him?"

"I certainly did not," he said vehemently.

Relief flooded through me as I realized that Mr. Darcy had not poisoned his friend against Jane.

"Then why did it take so long for you to come to Hertfordshire," I blurted out. "Why did Caroline's letters leave Jane feeling as though you would never have any intention to see her at all?"

He sighed heavily. "My sister-- That is a story for another time. But arranging to come to Hertfordshire was not a simple task. Nor was closing up our houses in London, or managing the sale of another... Darcy is the one who saw to it all. I haven't the head for such things. But he has done as he promised, and it is all done now. I hope your sister, and you, can forgive my absence."

I paused for just a moment to punish him, and enjoyed the brief flash of panic in his blue eyes as he wondered if I would reply.

"There will be nothing to forgive when I see the smile on my sister's face while you are dancing," I said brightly.

Mr. Bingley's laughter echoed through the room and Jane looked over immediately. Without an apology, she left her dance partner standing in the middle of the floor and rushed toward Mr. Bingley. I released my hold on his elbow and stepped away as my sister approached.

They deserved their moment, and my heart was swollen with happiness for them.

But, just as they were about to embrace, I looked behind me to see another man standing in the doorway.

Mr. Darcy.

"Miss Bennet," Mr. Darcy said, "I do hope you will grace me with a few moments of your time?"

"I... I believe my Mama is looking for me," I said quickly. "You must forgive me."

His smile was brief, chest tightened to see it. *Why had he come?*

"Miss Bennet," he said gently. "It is you who must forgive me. I have much to apologize for, and all I ask is that you will listen to what I have to say."

I nodded. "I should like a glass of punch," I said. "If I am to listen to you after the way you last spoke to me at Pemberley, I will need something to drink."

"As you wish," he replied and offered his elbow to me.

I placed my hand on his arm and let him lead me to the tables of rum punch.

His hand was warm as he placed it over mine.

He led me through the crowd to the punch table and lifted a drink for me. I took a sip, and the cold liquid felt soothing against my throat.

"Miss Bennet," Mr. Darcy began. "I-- I must beg your forgiveness for how I spoke to you at Pemberley. In the gardens... It was shameful of me, and I have regretted it every moment of every day since your carriage departed."

I didn't know what he wanted me to say. Did I forgive him?

"I cannot forgive you if I do not know that your opinion has changed," I choked out.

He nodded. "You are right to deny me forgiveness," he said. "It was Charles who told me that I was being hardheaded and foolish. That I should weigh the deeper value against the surface..."

"My family is still poor," I said sharply.

"And I am still a fool," he replied. "I have thought of nothing but you since that night in the garden. And I will

think of nothing else until the last day of my life. Whether
you forgive me or not, I love you, Elizabeth. Most ardently.
And I shall not stop. But if you do not accept my apology,
then I shall depart this place and you will never see me
again."

His words stabbed deep into my heart.

Never see him again?

Was I truly so angry?

"Charles charged me to think about what I wanted from
the woman who would become the Mistress of Pemberley...
and as I spent hours and days alone on the estate, I knew that
I wanted hours and days filled with laughter, furious
opinions, and... you."

"Oh--"

"But if you will not have me, I shall leave tonight, and you
will not have to think of me, or of avoiding me, ever again."

"I--"

His dark eyes were so sincere, the warmth of his hand so
gentle on mine. I wanted to believe that he had changed. I
wanted to believe that he had taken his friend's words to
heart.

"You are the one who arranged for Mr. Bingley to take
Netherfield Park?"

He inclined his head. "I did. I had my solicitor look into
the property as soon as I discovered where you were from.
That Charles was so taken with your sister was... it was very
fortunate, indeed."

"Indeed," I murmured. "And my family?"

"What of them?"

"You do not approve of them--fortune hunters in search of
wealthy husbands for the other daughters?"

I had not wanted to think about the shouts I had

overheard that night at Pemberley. But they had been clear enough as though he had been shouting his accusations directly at me.

"I shall happily assist in putting them in the path of other rich gentlemen," he said with a smile that made me laugh.

It was as though he had heard my mother's most fervent wishes.

"Mama will adore you for that," I said. "And have you spoken to my father?"

"I have not," he said. "But Charles tells me that he is a pleasant fellow, and I feel certain that I shall enjoy his company immensely. But, Elizabeth... I have come here to ask for your permission to court you. I hope that you believe that I would not come if I did not have the greatest regard for your person, and the deepest respect for your character. I know I have given you no reason to trust me, or to believe that I could change, but I can promise you my steadfast loyalty, with an affection that is unlikely to fade."

"But--"

A smile tugged at his lips. "If you will not give me your permission, I shall wait until spring and then ask again."

Surprise coursed through me, and then a very different emotion as tears pricked my eyelashes and threatened to spill down my cheeks.

"I accept your apology," I said. "And you have my permission..."

His eyebrow lifted in surprise. "I do?"

I nodded. "I must confess that I thought my heart to be too broken by your rejection to ever be mended... but I can admit now that I love you."

"I love you too, Elizabeth," he said, and then he lifted my hand to his lips and kissed it. His lips were soft, but his eyes were filled with the joy of a man on the brink of the greatest happiness.

I felt it.

In fact, I knew it.

With that simple kiss, chaste and full of promise, I knew that I was the luckiest woman in the world. He *had* changed, and I knew that I would ever have reason to doubt him again.

THE END

ALSO FROM BLUE FLOWERS PRESS

An Almost Forgotten Love

The Cruelest Season

A Blushing Bride

A Troublesome Tenant

A Season of Love

A Missed Engagement

Unapologetically, Elizabeth

Officer Darcy

An Unexpected Joy

Elizabeth's Deception

MERYTON MYSTERIES

The Trouble with Lords

The Trouble with Officers

Run Away to Pemberley ~ A Pride & Prejudice Coloring Book